FLICKA

Untamed Spirit

D1377508

FOX 2000 PICTURES PRESENTS A GIL NETTER PRODUCTION "FLICKA" ALISON LOHMAN TIM McGRAW MARIA BELLO COSTUME DESIGNER MOLLY MAGINNIS MUSIC SUPERVISOR JASON ALEXANDER MUSIC BY AARON ZIGMAN CO-PRODUCER KEVIN HALLORAN FILM EDITOR ANDREW MARCUS PRODUCTION DESIGNER SHARON SEYMOUR DIRECTOR OF PHOTOGRAPHY J. MICHAEL MURO PRODUCED BY GIL NETTER BASED UPON THE NOVEL "MY FRIEND FLICKA" BY MARY O'HARA SCREENPLAY BY MARK ROSENTHAL & LAWRENCE KONNER DIRECTED BY MICHAEL MAYER

www.flickamovie.com

© 2006 Twentieth Century Fox

HarperCollins®, ☛®, and HarperKidsEntertainment™ are trademarks of HarperCollins Publishers.

Flicka: Untamed Spirit
Fkicka ™ and © 2006 Twentieth Century Fox Film Corporation. All rights reserved.
Printed in the United States of America.
No part of this book may be used or reproduced in any manner whatsoever without
written permission except in the case of brief quotations embodied in critical articles and reviews. For
information address HarperCollins Children's Books, a division of HarperCollins Publishers,
1350 Avenue of the Americas, New York, NY 10019.
www.harperchildrens.com

Library of Congress catalog card number: 2005933587
ISBN-10: 0-06-087607-7 — ISBN-13: 978-0-06-087607-4

Typography by Scott Richards
1 2 3 4 5 6 7 8 9 10
❖
First Edition

FLICKA
Untamed Spirit

Written by JUDY KATSCHKE

Based on the Motion Picture

Screenplay by

MARK ROSENTHAL

& LAWRENCE KONNER

Based upon the novel

"My Friend Flicka" by MARY O'HARA

HarperKidsEntertainment
An Imprint of HarperCollins*Publishers*

FLICKA

Untamed Spirit

CHAPTER ONE

Creeeak!

Katy McLaughlin froze on the squeaky step. She held her riding boots—and her breath. The last thing she wanted to do was wake up her family—especially her dad!

Katy quietly tiptoed down the stairs. She stopped to gaze at her favorite painting on the wall. It showed a herd of wild horses galloping across a plain. Katy loved horses and would do anything to ride one—even if it meant sneaking out of the house at the crack of dawn!

When Katy reached the front door, she opened it carefully. The doorknob slipped from her hand and—*slam!* Katy gritted her teeth. She sat on the porch, pulled on her riding boots, and tore off across Goose Creek Ranch.

Katy's heavy boots didn't keep her from running like the wind. It was her first day of summer vacation. It was also her first day home from the Laramie Academy, the fancy boarding school in Wyoming that her parents sent her to.

But sneaking out for a ride wasn't Katy's only secret. Her other secret was stuffed inside the pocket of her denim jacket.

Katy shuddered as she remembered the letter.

"Katy McLaughlin," one of the prefects told her yesterday in school. "You need to see the headmaster."

"Thank you." Katy gulped as she took the white envelope with the gold school crest. She didn't have to open it to know what was inside. It was a letter to her parents that said she was flunking school.

Katy was going to give her dad the letter when he picked her up at the van stop. But Rob McLaughlin was as tough as the saddle he rode every day, so Katy didn't have the guts. And she didn't have the heart to tell her mom, Nell. It was Nell McLaughlin's idea to send Katy to private school in the first place. Katy's older brother, Howard, knew by the look in her eyes that something was wrong.

"How bad can it be?" Howard had whispered.

"Worse," Katy whispered back.

Katy switched her thoughts from school to the stable. As she burst into the horse barn, twenty heads turned in their stalls.

"Who feels like running?" Katy asked.

In no time, Katy was riding bareback on Yankee, a handsome chestnut gelding. The horse jumped over the pasture gate. After dashing across the meadow, Yankee splashed through the waters of Goose Creek. Katy gripped Yankee's thick mane as he galloped up a steep mountainside.

"Whoa!" Katy called.

Yankee slowed down on the summit. Katy reached into her pocket and pulled out the crumpled letter.

"What am I going to do?" Katy sighed. She still didn't get it. When it came to riding, she was fearless. When it came to her dad, she was a total wimp!

Yankee let out a snort and began to buck.

Something must have spooked him, Katy thought. She stroked his mane gently and said, "Stop it."

Yankee kicked up his hooves. With a whinny he raced down the steep incline, bucking all the way.

At the base of the mountain, Yankee shot

into the woods. It was dark and thick with trees and bushes.

"You want to go home, huh, Yankee?" Katy asked. "At least somebody does."

Suddenly Katy heard a deep rumbling sound. She brought Yankee to a halt and sat perfectly still. It was the sound of a mountain lion!

"Quiet, Yankee," Katy whispered.

A shadow moved in the brush. Yankee raised his front hooves, tossing Katy to the ground. Katy stood up. But just as she was about to remount, Yankee sped off into the woods.

Katy stiffened as she stood alone. A pair of yellow eyes glowed at her from the shadows. Running away was a bad idea. But when the bushes began to shake, Katy couldn't think of a better one!

Katy spun around and ran for her life. Thorns and brambles scraped her arms and face. Her long hair wrapped around a sticky shrub.

"Owww!" Katy cried. She twisted her body

until her hair came free. She ran forward until the tip of her boot snagged on a large rock.

Katy pitched forward, landing facedown in a field of wildflowers. She glanced up and her eyes opened wider. Standing a few feet away was a long-legged black mustang, her mane matted with burrs and nettles!

The horse cried out and raised her front legs. She wielded her hooves in the air. Then she began charging straight toward Katy.

"Don't hurt me!" Katy shouted.

CHAPTER TWO

Katy rolled on the ground and covered her head with her arms. She could hear hooves stampeding in the dirt. She thought she was history until she heard the hooves running past her.

Katy glanced up. The mustang wasn't charging her. She was charging the mountain lion!

The cat growled at the rearing mustang. Then it backed off slowly into the woods.

"You scared it away!" Katy said excitedly.

The horse whinnied and headed toward Katy!

"No!" Katy cried as she dove to the side.

The mustang thundered past her, down the mountainside.

Katy jumped to her feet. Her face was cut and her hair was tangled. But she knew she

was very lucky. If it weren't for the mustang, she would have been lion-chow for sure!

Katy ran all the way back to the ranch. She could smell pancakes and sausages as she pulled open the screen door and raced into the kitchen. Seated at the long table were Katy's parents, Howard, and Jack and Gus, the ranch hands.

"A lion!" Katy exclaimed. "On the mountain!"

"You're bleeding!" Nell exclaimed. She ran to the sink for a wet cloth.

"A mustang, Dad!" Katy went on. "It scared off the lion!"

"Slow down," Rob said. "Which was it? A lion or a horse?"

Katy sat in a chair as her mom dabbed her face. "Both!" she said. "Aren't you going to do something?"

Jack grinned goofily and said, "Did you see Sasquatch, too?"

Katy glared at Jack. "Did someone ask your opinion?" she snapped.

Gus frowned at Jack as he reached for the maple syrup. He always loved Katy like a daughter. He even liked calling her "flicka," a Swedish word meaning pretty young girl.

"Would a lion come that close?" Nell asked. "Would it attack the ranch?"

"Lions will attack anything," Rob answered.

"It *was* a lion. Honest!" Katy insisted.

Rob raised an eyebrow at Katy. "As long as we're being honest," he said. "Is there something you need to tell me about school?"

"School?" Katy tensed up.

Rob pulled a letter from his pocket. He unfolded it and held it up. When Katy saw the school crest, her stomach flipped. She and her brother traded nervous glances.

I am so busted, Katy thought.

"The headmaster faxed this," Rob said. "It says they gave you the topic for your final essay in advance. It was 'How the West Was Settled.' But you handed in a blank test book."

"I wrote it in my head," Katy explained. "I just didn't get a chance to put it down on paper."

"In your head," Rob repeated with a sigh.

Katy knew it sounded like a lame answer. But it was the total truth.

"They just want us to spit back what they tell us!" Katy complained. "But my opinion isn't their opinion."

"Their opinion is that you should repeat the year," Rob said. "Throw it away like money down the drain!"

Rob rattled off the farm's expenses: the generator that needed replacing, the new barn roof they needed, the vacation trip they never took just so Katy could go to a fancy boarding school.

"I go along," Rob said, "because your mother wants you to go to college."

"Your father wants it, too," Nell insisted.

"Now she might not even graduate high school!" Rob exclaimed.

"You can go to your brother's school, Katy." Jack laughed. "The University of Manual Labor!"

That did it! Katy sprung out of her chair and lunged at Jack.

"Just teasing!" Jack said. He tried to hold Katy off, but she was strong.

"Enough!" Rob snapped. "We've got a fence line to repair and a mound of manure to spread."

Chairs scraped the floor as the men stood

up. Jack grabbed two more pancakes on his way out of the kitchen.

Nell put her arm around Katy's shoulders, but Katy wasn't worried about school anymore. She was worried about the wild mustang that saved her life.

I have to find her, Katy thought.

She pulled away from her mother and dashed outside. The men were busy loading fence posts into a truck.

"Dad?" Katy asked.

"I'm counting, Katy," Rob said, not looking her way. "That's twenty, twenty-two, twenty-four—"

"I think we should bring that mustang in," Katy said. "I could probably find her."

"No," Rob said.

"I'll help," Howard called from the truck.

"This doesn't concern you!" Rob snapped.

Howard's shoulders dropped. Rob turned to Katy and said, "If you live on a ranch, you have to pitch in. Do your chores, help your mother, and write that essay. Maybe I can talk the school into passing you."

"Yes, sir," Katy said.

She turned and trudged back to the house.

After a soak in the tub, Katy went straight to her room. She sprawled out on her bed and opened her notebook to a clean page. As she thought about the early American settlers, her mind drifted to the early American horse.

Katy always believed that the west was built on horses. Wherever a settler left a footprint there was a hoofprint. But the wild mustangs—or *mistengos*—always had a bad rap. They were hunted down by the hundreds and sold to slaughterhouses.

Katy gazed out her window. Somewhere in those mountains the wild mustang was running free. And if her dad wouldn't find the horse, Katy would. . . .

CHAPTER THREE

The following afternoon, Katy saddled Yankee up and rode him out of the barn. Her mom and dad were busy working and hadn't seen her slip out of the house. Now she was on her way to the woods to find the wild mustang.

Before the lion does, Katy thought.

Katy galloped Yankee down the mountain and into the woods. It was eerily quiet until Yankee stepped over a fallen tree and—*snap!*

Katy gasped as a black horse head popped up from the tall grass. It was the wild mustang!

The wild filly cried out. It jerked backward and galloped away.

Katy gave Yankee a kick. He bucked, whinnied, and then zigzagged through the woods after the mustang. Katy sat forward, clutching her rope. She refused to take her eyes off of the wild horse, even for a second.

As Yankee caught up to the mustang, Katy stood in the stirrups. She skillfully swung the

lasso. It slipped around the mustang's neck on the first try!

"Gotcha!" Katy said.

But the wild horse had other plans. It spun and reared in the air. Katy gripped the rope, but she was no match for the mustang's

strength. She pulled Katy off of her horse and dragged her away!

Katy dug her boot heels into the ground. As the mustang ran she stumbled and fell.

They broke through the trees onto the mountain slope and tumbled all the way down.

Meanwhile, at the base of the mountain, Rob and his ranch hands were rounding up a herd of grazing horses.

"Gus, Jack!" Rob shouted. "Keep them moving!"

Rob suddenly heard the sound of falling stones. He turned and saw a horse falling down the mountainside. As he looked closer, his jaw dropped.

"Katy?" Rob cried.

Katy was covered with dust as the mustang dragged her along the ground. Rob shouted at the mustang and beat its bucking legs with his rope. The horse finally broke away, leading the rest of the herd in a wild chase.

"Let them run it out, Dad," Howard said.

"Right," Rob said sarcastically. He leaped onto his horse and shot off after his herd.

Katy sat slumped on the ground. She could see the men roping the mustang and pulling her away from their own horses.

Katy hung her head. All she wanted to do was disappear—especially when the shadow of her dad loomed over her.

"I didn't want the lion to get my horse," Katy muttered.

"*Your* horse?" Rob cried. "That mangy beast doesn't belong to you or anybody. I'm surprised it's still alive!"

"What are you going to do with her?" Katy asked as she stood up.

"I don't want to do a thing with this *loco* creature," Rob said.

Katy frowned when she heard the Spanish word for crazy. Her dad didn't have a clue about mustangs. Just like he didn't have a clue about her!

"Isn't Norbert looking for wild mustangs?" Gus asked.

Norbert Rye was a rodeo manager in Wyoming. He was always on the lookout for bucking broncos.

"Let's get this horse behind a fence," Rob ordered. "But keep it away from the herd."

Katy watched as Gus and Jack struggled with the mustang's ropes. She would worry about the rodeo later. At least now they were taking her home.

"Come look at her, Mom!" Katy called.

Nell gasped as Rob towed the mustang into the ranch. "This is the horse Katy was talking about?" she asked.

The men pulled the mustang into a round pen with a high white fence. They slammed the gate shut and left her alone to buck, rear, and whinny.

Rob pushed back his cowboy hat. He wiped the sweat off his forehead with his sleeve and said, "This is one dangerous animal."

"She's just scared," Katy said. "She'll calm down once I start training her."

"This horse will never be ridden," Rob said. "I'm calling Norbert after dinner."

"No!" Katy said. "I can ride her."

"No, you can't," Rob said. "And nobody goes into that pen without my permission!"

Rob walked away. The others stayed behind to gaze at the wild mustang.

Katy knew that she and the horse had a lot

in common. They both had a wild streak. And they both wanted to run free.

"Calm down, Flicka," Katy said softly.

"You named her?" Nell asked.

"Flicka," Katy repeated. She turned to smile at Gus. "That's the word, isn't it?"

"Yes," Gus said. "Beautiful young girl."

"You got the *girl* part right," Jack joked. "As for beautiful . . ."

Katy ignored Jack. To her, Flicka was the most beautiful creature in the world.

I don't care what Dad says, Katy thought. *She's my horse and I'm going to ride her!*

CHAPTER FOUR

It was the middle of the night when Katy climbed the paddock fence. She could see Flicka charging back and forth in the moonlight.

If only Flicka knew me, Katy thought.

She leaned on the fence and hummed a soothing lullaby. Flicka stopped running—almost like magic!

Katy jumped down off the fence into the pen. She smiled at Flicka and said, "Hey, girl!"

Flicka snorted and charged straight toward Katy. Katy dove quickly under the fence.

"Sorry, girl," Katy said. "That was my fault."

Katy watched Flicka from behind the fence.

She had to gain this animal's trust. But how?

Suddenly Katy had a brainstorm.

She dashed to the barn and returned with her pockets stuffed with apples.

Katy climbed back into the paddock. She sang the lullaby as she carefully stepped forward.

Flicka trotted in a circle around the pen. She screeched to a stop when she saw the apple in Katy's hand.

"Come and get it," Katy called. "But you'll have to trust me first."

Flicka stepped closer and closer. She snatched an apple with her teeth from Katy's hand.

"You know me," Katy cooed as she stroked Flicka's mane. "Good girl."

Katy was on a mission. She would sneak out every night to train Flicka. She would show her father she could ride this horse.

But training a wild horse wasn't Katy's only problem. She knew it was hard for her parents to make ends meet. Real estate agents and developers were always trying to get her dad to sell the farm. She had a feeling he was really considering it now. Howard didn't care. His dream was to go to college and eventually move as far away as he could. But Katy wouldn't be able to bear losing the ranch.

How could Dad be so . . . so loco? Katy wondered.

Well, her dad might give up, but she wouldn't. Finally one night, after many nights of getting thrown, Katy jumped on Flicka's back and trotted her in a circle. She waited to be bucked off, but it didn't happen!

"Wait 'til Dad sees you now, Flicka!" Katy said. "Let's go."

Katy leaned over and released the latch on the paddock gate. She sang softly into Flicka's ear until the horse stepped through.

After an awesome ride across the pasture, Katy rode Flicka back to the paddock. She was

about to climb off when she noticed another horse, Rocket, outside the fence.

Flicka cried out.

"Let her be," Katy said softly.

More curious horses walked over. As they trotted around the fence, Rocket gave chase. That's when everything Katy taught Flicka seemed to fall apart.

"Whoa!" Katy cried as Flicka charged the fence. *"Whoooooa!"*

CHAPTER FIVE

Flicka bucked Katy off her back. Then the mustang crashed through the paddock fence and chased the other horses in the main corral. The sound of thundering hooves reached the barn and the house. Gus and Jack ran for the horses. Rob, Nell, and Howard ran straight to Katy.

"Are you hurt?" Rob asked.

"No," Katy muttered as she stood up.

"You couldn't plan a better way to get killed," Rob said.

"Rob, don't . . ." Nell pleaded.

"Flicka just wants to learn, Daddy," Katy said.

"How do you know anything about that creature?" Rob demanded.

"Because we're the same!" Katy declared.

The McLaughlins stayed quiet for a moment. Then Rob said, between gritted teeth, "I won't have that horse on my ranch!"

"You don't get it," Katy shouted as she raced to the house. "You don't get anything!"

The next morning, Katy came out to the barn to find her worst nightmare was coming true. Norbert Rye and her dad were loading

Flicka into a trailer. Her mom and Howard stood by, watching in silence.

"You can't take her!" Katy shouted, charging at Norbert.

"It's better this way, Katy," Rob said.

Flicka kicked against the trailer wall.

"She's never been inside a trailer before!" Katy said. "She's scared!"

"She'll be fine, sweetie," Norbert said. "She's going to be a rodeo star."

Katy yanked at the trailer gate. When Rob pulled her back she pummeled him with her fists.

"You're not my father anymore!" Katy shouted.

"Flicka should stay here," Howard piped in.

"Stay out of this," Rob warned. "Until you're running this ranch, I'll make the decisions."

"I don't *want* to run your ranch," Howard said. "I'm sick of this place. I've given it a lot of thought and guess what? I'm never going to be a rancher. I want to go college."

Katy stared at her brother. He had never spoken up to their father before. It was about time! She'd been waiting forever for Howard to confess his real dream to their dad.

"I'm sorry you feel that way," Rob said flatly. "Norbert, take your horse away."

Norbert tipped his cowboy hat and jumped into the trailer.

As he drove off, Katy gave chase. She could hear Flicka kicking the trailer walls. Norbert picked up speed and Katy fell back. She turned to glare at her father. Then she shot off for the pasture.

As Katy ran, she thought about the wild

mustang's place in American history. No one really wanted them. They just wanted them to disappear, just as her dad wanted Flicka to disappear.

Katy stopped running and caught her breath, her mind filled with visions of wild horses. She decided it was time to head back.

As soon as she reached the house, Katy went to her room, sat down at her desk, and began writing through a blur of tears.

CHAPTER SIX

"Should we tell her, Miranda?" Howard asked.

Katy stopped splashing in the pond. She and her brother and his girlfriend, Miranda Koop, had taken the afternoon off from doing chores in order to go swimming. Katy knew Miranda from school. She was an awesome rodeo rider.

"Tell me what?" Katy asked.

"Miranda saw Flicka," Howard spilled the beans.

"Where?" Katy demanded.

"At the fairgrounds," Miranda said. "When I was practicing the course."

Katy's heart pounded. For the last few days

all Katy could think about was Flicka! "How did she look?" Katy asked excitedly.

Miranda hesitated. After a moment she said, "Those horses Flicka was with scared me. And I'm never scared of horses."

Katy frowned as she flipped onto her back. As she floated on the water, she realized she had to rescue Flicka.

"There's a prize to ride Flicka in the rodeo," Miranda added. "Over eight thousand dollars."

Katy dove under the water. When she popped up she declared, "I can win that race! I want to ride Flicka!"

"You're demented!" Howard cried. "And you're too young anyway."

"*You're* not!" Katy said, a plan forming in her head instantly. "You enter the race and I ride Flicka. Then I buy Flicka back with the prize money."

Howard and Miranda stared at Katy as if she were from another planet.

"Flicka isn't Dad's horse anymore," Katy

went on. "And if he tries to sell our land, I'll buy that, too!"

"Katy, she's way too dangerous to ride," Howard said.

"I only have to stay on for a few seconds," Katy explained. "I've already done that!" She looked at Miranda for support.

Miranda laughed and then nodded.

"I don't know," Howard said, shaking his head. "It's a crazy plan."

"Yeah," Katy said. She gave her brother a splash. "So crazy it's got to work!"

A few nights later, Katy stood in front of her dresser mirror. She tucked her hair inside a cowboy hat. Then she slipped on heavy work-gloves and struck a tough pose. The rodeo was the next day and Katy was going to win back her horse. No one would ever know she was too young to compete.

CHAPTER SEVEN

"Wow!" Katy said as she walked through the fairgrounds. It seemed like half of Wyoming had shown up for the big rodeo.

A livestock auction was in full swing, as was a tractor pull, Indian dancing, and bungee jumping over a mud-filled hog slop.

Katy's cowboy clothes were waiting for her in Miranda's horse trailer. As she changed, Miranda and Howard were having second thoughts about the whole thing.

"Can we rethink this?" Howard asked.

"No way," Katy said. "If you don't want to do it, I'll do it myself."

Katy swaggered out in her cowboy hat,

jean jacket, and work gloves. Just one thing was missing. . . .

"Hold on," Howard said. He picked up a handful of dirt and smeared it over Katy's face. Now she looked like a real rodeo rider.

While Howard registered for the event, Katy looked around for her parents. She hoped they were busy at the food tent or watching the tractor pull—anything to keep them away from the wild horse corral!

Katy checked out the other teams as they gathered outside the corral. All of the cowboys towered over Katy. And they made sure she knew it. . . .

"Rules say you can put a baby cradle on the horse?" one rider teased.

Katy tuned out the laughing cowboys. As long as they couldn't tell her age, everything was cool.

"Okay!" a man holding a clipboard called. "Shout 'em out!"

The cowboys rushed to the fence to call out their choice of horses:

"The chestnut!"

"The blaze!"

"The paint!"

Katy jabbed Howard with her elbow.

"Um," Howard blurted, "we'll take the black filly."

"Son, you just lost this race," the man said. "That horse is truly *loco*."

Katy rolled her eyes.

"Ladies and gentlemen and cowboys!" a voice on the loudspeaker boomed. "The wild horse race is about to start. Enter at your own risk!"

"Let's go," Katy told Howard.

On their way to the gate, Katy spotted Norbert. He was in the stands, staring right at them.

"I hope he didn't recognize me," Katy whispered.

The crowd *yahoo*ed as wild horses were led into the chute.

"Look at those devils!" the announcer said. "Let's bring out the first set of victims—I mean cowboys!"

The first teams marched into the ring. The hold gates swung open and wild horses thundered out.

Katy, Howard, and Miranda watched from outside the fence. Beefy cowboys were being kicked, thrown, and dragged around the ring like rag dolls!

"Let's hear it for our winners." The announcer laughed. "Oh, wait. There are none!"

It was time for the next set of contestants. The gate swung open and Katy and Howard entered the ring.

"Four, three, two, one!"

43

More wild horses bounded into the ring. When Katy saw Flicka her eyes lit up.

"Flicka!" Katy called.

Flicka snorted as Katy and Howard ran over.

"You know me, girl," Katy said softly. "I'm your friend. And I'll set you free."

Flicka's hooves crashed down. Katy rested

her cheek against Flicka's head. Softly she sang their favorite lullaby.

Howard held Flicka still. Katy was about to swing the saddle onto her back when Howard whispered, "Omigosh—they're here!"

Katy whirled around. Her dad was pushing his way through the crowd toward the fence!

"Norbert must have told him we were here," Howard said.

Katy's heart sank as she clutched the saddle. "What was I thinking?" She groaned. "Dad will *never* let me keep Flicka."

This time it was Howard who refused to give up. "Just win, Katy!" he said.

It won't make any difference to Dad, Katy thought.

She dropped the saddle, grabbed Flicka's mane, and leaped onto her bare back. Just then, a spinning mare crossed their path. Spooked, Flicka bucked, reared, and began to charge.

Katy stayed focused as she steered Flicka toward the barrels. "Run, girl!" she shouted.

The crowd cheered as Flicka rocketed between the barrels. Katy rode her past the judges. She rode her past the crowd and past her father.

"I won't let them take us, girl!" Katy said. She gave Flicka a kick. The black mustang charged through the gate and out of the ring.

"Pull up! Pull up!" Howard shouted.

Katy and Flicka raced past the crowd and into the parking lot. Then Katy rode Flicka out of the fairgrounds.

Rob and Howard watched in horror as Katy
disappeared into the darkness.

CHAPTER EIGHT

"This is our creek, isn't it, girl?" Katy asked.

Flicka whinnied as she bobbed her sopping-wet mane. It had begun to storm and the rain was gushing down in sheets.

"If we cross the low bank we can follow it home," Katy said. She didn't know if that was good or bad.

"He's going to be mad at us, Flicka," Katy said. "But we showed him!"

Flicka stopped short.

"What is it, girl?" Katy asked. She leaned forward and listened. Through the rain she heard a low growling noise. Two yellow eyes glowed out from a dark shadow. Katy's blood froze. It was the mountain lion!

The shadow disappeared in a flash of lightning. Katy heard the growl again. Another flash of lightning revealed the lion crouching on a tree branch. The lion crept forward, ready to spring.

Flicka snorted as she charged the lion. Katy lost her grip and tumbled to the ground. She watched in horror as the lion jumped on Flicka, digging its sharp claws into the mustang's back.

Katy picked up a handful of rocks. She hurled them at the lion and screamed, "Get away from her!"

The lion ran away.

Flicka wobbled on her long legs. Then she sank to her knees and collapsed to the ground.

"Flicka!" Katy cried. She ran to Flicka and cradled her head. "Get up, Flicka. The lion is going to come back!"

But Flicka wouldn't move.

"Somebody help me!" Katy shouted. *"Please!"*

Rob, Nell, Howard, and Jack were wrapped in slickers and riding their horses up the mountainside. Flashlights were tied to saddles, but the heavy rain made it impossible to see.

"Katy! Where are you?" Nell shouted.

Rob steered his horse toward the creek. He called Katy's name as he weaved through the cottonwoods. Suddenly two dark shapes appeared on the ground. As Rob rode closer he saw Katy and Flicka.

"Katy!" Rob shouted. He jumped off his horse and lifted Katy into his arms. By now Katy was shivering hard.

"I told you there was a lion, Daddy," Katy said.

Katy was rushed to the ranch house. By the time she was put to bed, she had a raging fever of 105. The storm was raging, too, so there was no way to get Katy to a doctor or a hospital.

Images of Flicka drifted through Katy's feverish head. She knew what was done to injured horses. They were shot.

"Flicka . . ." Katy murmured.

Downstairs, Gus and Jack were returning from the mountain. The news about Flicka was grim.

"The mustang is in pretty bad shape," Gus said.

"Go back and put her down," Rob ordered.

"But Katy will hear the shot!" Jack argued.

"She'll think its thunder," Rob said.

"No, she won't," Jack said. "Katy is smart."

"She'll know it's Flicka," Gus agreed.

Rob shook his head. "I can't let that animal suffer," he said. "I'll do it myself."

Rob went to his bedroom for his Winchester rifle. As he carried it out, he saw Katy standing in the hall. Her face was covered with sweat. Her eyes were two sunken holes as she stared at the shotgun.

"Are you going to kill Flicka?" Katy asked weakly.

"I'm just going to take a look at her," Rob said.

Nell rushed over and guided Katy back to bed. But Katy didn't care about her fever. How could she live without Flicka?

Clutching the gun, Rob rode his horse up the mountainside. As he rode along the high bank he heard Flicka whimpering. Through the rain he could see the mustang spread out on the ground.

Rob climbed down from his horse. With a tear in his eye he aimed the gun and planted his finger on the trigger. But just as he was about to pull it, Flicka struggled to stand up!

Rob stared at Flicka over his gun. It was as if the mustang was fighting for her own life!

"It's up to you, girl," Rob whispered.

Both horses whinnied. Rob's horse turned and broke into a run.

Rob didn't know what spooked the horses until he looked up and saw the mountain lion crouching in a tree. As the lion lunged, Rob aimed the gun and fired.

The gunshot echoed down the mountain to the ranch house. Katy shuddered as the sound exploded in her head.

"Flicka!" Katy cried.

CHAPTER NINE

Rob dabbed Katy's feverish face with a wet washcloth. His eyes were filled with tears as he watched his only daughter fade away.

"I promise to tell you every day that I'm so proud you're my daughter," Rob pleaded. "Just stay here, Katy. Please."

Katy's eyes remained shut. Rob wrung the washcloth over a basin. Then he stood up and left Katy to sleep.

Walking past Katy's desk, Rob saw her notebook. He picked it up and flipped through it. There on the pages was Katy's school essay, "How the West Was Settled."

Rob sat down and read every page. Then he turned on the computer and typed Katy's essay, word for word.

When Nell came into the room she found Rob fast asleep at Katy's desk. Tears filled Nell's eyes as she read Katy's essay on the computer screen and saw that it was ready to go to the headmaster of Katy's school. She pulled over the keyboard and pressed Send.

Katy's eyes blinked open. She could see her father standing at the window. His eyes were closed and his head was bowed to his chest.

"What's wrong, Daddy?" Katy asked.

Rob whirled around. When he saw Katy sitting up in bed he ran to touch her forehead.

"Fever's down!" Rob declared.

Katy's dry lips quivered as she began to cry. "It's my fault Flicka is dead," she said.

"I don't think so," Rob said. He wrapped Katy in a blanket and carried her outside to the porch. The rain had stopped and the sun was shining brightly.

Rob gave a whistle. Katy had no idea what was going on. Then she saw her mom come out from behind the barn leading the beautiful black mustang!

"Flicka," Katy said softly.

Rob carried Katy over to Flicka. Nell and Howard smiled as Katy pressed her hand gently on Flicka's neck.

"Your mom has been taking good care of her for the past few days," Rob said. "But when you're better I expect you to care for her yourself."

"But—" Katy said. "You said if I don't get back into school—"

"Dad sent your essay," Howard cut in.

"I told them I didn't know much about writing," Rob explained. "But I sure know

about the west!"

"What did they say?" Katy asked.

Nell folded her arms across her chest. "What does anyone say to your father?" she asked with a grin.

"Yes, sir!" Howard laughed.

For the first time in days Katy laughed, too. With Flicka alive and back at the ranch she felt happier than ever before.

And when Katy was well enough to gallop her horse across the valley and up the mountainside—all she could feel was *free*!